This igloo book belongs to:

....

Published in 2019
by Igloo Books Ltd
Cottage Farm
Sywell
NN6 0BJ
www.igloobooks.com

Igloo Books is an imprint of Bonnier Books UK

1019 003
6 8 10 11 9 7
ISBN 978-1-78197-622-7

Illustrated by Jo Parry

Printed and manufactured in China

Little Mouse's
New Friend

igloobooks

It was the first day of school and all the animals were **very** excited. "I can't wait to meet my new classmates," said Little Mouse, **skipping** alongside his mum. "It's going to be **SO** much fun!"

Hetty the hedgehog came through the school gate with her mum. She wasn't excited about starting school at all. While Little Mouse and the others chatted noisily, Hetty **tip-toed** past, hoping no one would notice her.

When the bell rang, everyone filed into the classroom and Hetty accidentally bumped into Owl. **"Ouch!"** he cried. "You **pricked** me with your spikes." "Sorry," squeaked Hetty. "I didn't mean to."

Classroom 1

Hetty felt upset. Her sharp spikes made her
different from all the other animals.
"I wish I was **soft** and **smooth** like everyone
else," she thought, **patting** down her spikes.

In the classroom, everyone quickly found a seat, except for Hetty. The only place left was next to Owl, who **scowled** and crossed his wings, **grumpily**.

All the way through the lesson, Hetty and Owl sat in silence. When lunchtime came, everyone ran outside to play together, but Hetty stayed sitting in her seat, looking **very** sad.

"What's wrong, Hetty?" asked Mrs Bunny.
"Don't you want to play with the others?"
"No one will want to play with me," replied Hetty.
"I'm too **sharp** and **prickly**."

"Your spikes make you **special!**" said Mrs Bunny, smiling. "Being different is a **good** thing. My ears are much longer than anybody else's, but I like them **very** much!"

After talking to Mrs Bunny, Hetty felt **much** better. She **loved** Mrs Bunny's extra-long ears and thought that maybe her own spikes weren't so bad after all. So, she decided to go outside and play.

On her way, Hetty overheard Owl talking to Little Mouse and he wasn't being very nice. "I **don't want** to play with you," said Owl, grumpily. "You're **far** too small to be any fun."

Hetty thought about what Mrs Bunny had told her
and decided to say something to Owl.
She felt **proud** to be spiky and she thought that
Little Mouse should be **proud** to be small.

"Leave him alone!" cried Hetty, to Owl.

"You shouldn't be mean just because someone
is different," added Hetty.
Owl **scowled** at Hetty and flew off, thinking
about what she had said.

"**Thanks,**" said Little Mouse, smiling at Hetty.
"It was really brave of you to say that to Owl.
I'm Little Mouse, what's your name?"
"I'm Hetty," said the little hedgehog with a **smile**.

Little Mouse looked at Hetty's spikes.
She certainly **wasn't** soft and smooth at all.
"Your spikes are so **cool!**" he said.
"Why don't you come and show them to my friends?"

Hetty felt a bit shy about meeting Little Mouse's fluffy friends, but everyone **loved** her spikes.

They all agreed that sticking up for Little Mouse was a very **brave** thing to do indeed.

Soon, Hetty had made **lots** of new friends.

Hetty, Little Mouse and the others had **lots** of fun playing games together that lunchtime.

Hetty soon forgot **all** about her spikes.

Little Mouse felt just as **big** as everybody else.

In the middle of their games, Hetty suddenly
noticed that Owl was all by himself.
"Come and play with us, Owl," she called.
"We need someone with **big**, **strong** wings
to play the superhero."

Owl happily flew over to join everyone.
He was sorry for being so mean before.
From across the playground, Mrs Bunny spotted
them and **waved** at Hetty with a **smile**.
She knew they would all be great friends.

When the bell **rang** at the end of the day,
Little Mouse, Hetty and the other animals couldn't
wait to see their mums and dads and tell them all
about their great first day at school.

Before she left, Hetty ran over to say goodbye to Little Mouse. "Can we play together again tomorrow?" she asked, hopefully. "I've had such a **good time!**"

"**Of course!**" said Little Mouse, happily.
"I'm so happy to have made a **new friend!**"